Mrs. McMurphy's Pumpkin

By
Rick Walton
Illustrated by
Delana Bettoli

HarperFestival®
A Division of HarperCollins*Publishers*

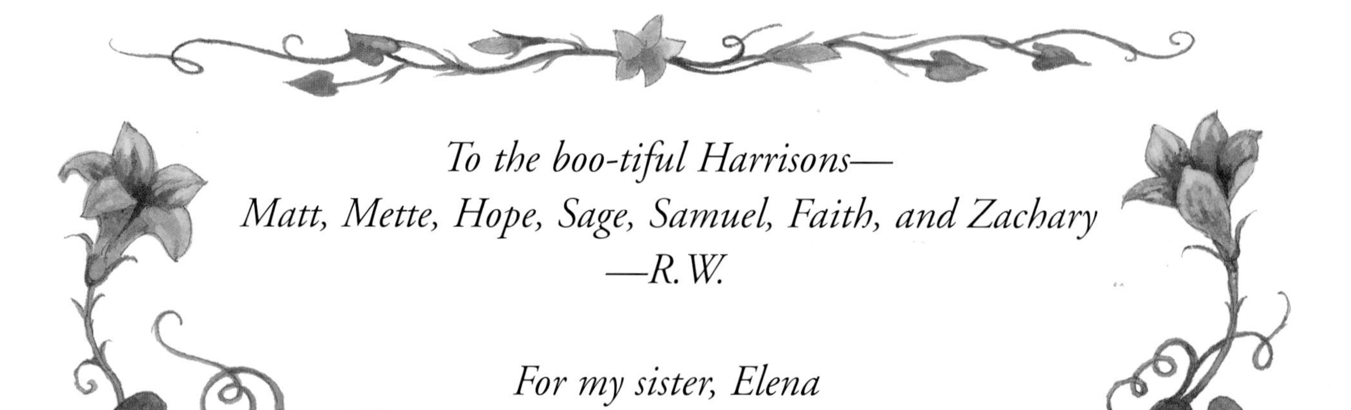

To the boo-tiful Harrisons—
Matt, Mette, Hope, Sage, Samuel, Faith, and Zachary
—R. W.

For my sister, Elena
—D.B.

The art was made with gouache paint and acrylic accents on watercolor paper.
Manufactured in China by South China Printing Company Ltd.

www.harperchildrens.com
Library of Congress catalog card number: 2003101049
Typography by Rick Farley
1 2 3 4 5 6 7 8 9 10
❖
First Edition

Mrs. McMurphy lived by herself on a farm at the edge of the woods.

Every morning she hushed her chickens, then sang to them as she fed them and gathered their eggs.

Every morning she gave hay to the cows, scratched them behind their ears, then told them to mind themselves while she milked.

And every morning she slopped the pigs, smiled at them, and said, "If you break out of your pens today, you're bacon!" Then she'd give them each a kiss and a pat.

One morning, four days before Halloween, Mrs. McMurphy got up to gather eggs, and found a large pumpkin with a wicked, wicked grin sitting in the hall by her front door.

And the pumpkin said, “My mouth is here. I speak to you. When my teeth are here, I’ll eat you!”

“What a sweet-looking pumpkin,” said Mrs. McMurphy, “but pumpkins belong outside.”

And she carried it out to the porch.

Three days before Halloween, Mrs. McMurphy got up to milk her cows, and found a large pumpkin with a wicked, wicked grin and a crooked nose sitting on her sofa.

And the pumpkin said, “My nose is here. I smell you. When my teeth are here, I’ll eat you!”

“Morning is my work time,” said Mrs. McMurphy. “Why don’t you come back in the afternoon? We’ll have cookies and milk.”

And she carried the pumpkin out and put it in the shed.

OCTOBER
29

Two days before Halloween, Mrs. McMurphy got up to feed her pigs, and found a large pumpkin with a wicked, wicked grin and a crooked nose and two pointy ears sitting in her kitchen doorway.

And the pumpkin said, "My ears are here. I hear you. When my teeth are here, I'll eat you!"

"Now, now," she said. "Let's remember our manners."

And she took the pumpkin outside
and set it floating down the river.

On the day before Halloween, Mrs. McMurphy got up to clean her house, and found a large pumpkin with a wicked, wicked grin and a crooked nose and two pointy ears and two mean eyes sitting on her kitchen counter.

And the pumpkin said, "My eyes are here. I see you. When my teeth are here, I'll eat you!"

"And what lovely eyes they are," she said, "but I'm afraid no one's allowed on my kitchen counter."

And she put the pumpkin in a
box and mailed it to the North Pole.

On Halloween morning, Mrs. McMurphy woke up to do her baking, and found a large pumpkin with a wicked, wicked grin and a crooked nose and two pointy ears and two mean eyes and large, sharp teeth sitting on her stove.

And the pumpkin said, "My teeth are here. I can bite you. It's time for me TO EAT YOU!"

"Oh!" said Mrs. McMurphy. "We'll have to see about that."

And that night, when ghosts and monsters and little princesses stopped at her door, Mrs. McMurphy fed them each a thick slice of warm, sweet . . .

pumpkin pie.